THE
ITSY BITSY
SPIDER

THE
ITSY BITSY
SPIDER

As told and illustrated by
Iza Trapani

Whispering Coyote Press
Dallas

*A huge thanks to Kim and Dan Adlerman for their
input and enthusiasm in producing this book*

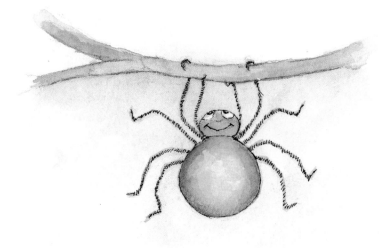

Published by Whispering Coyote Press
300 Crescent Court, Suite 860
Dallas, TX 75201
Copyright © 1993 by Iza Trapani
Printed in Hong Kong
Book production and design by Our House

13 14 15 16 17 18 19 20

Library of Congress Cataloging-in-Publication Data

Trapani, Iza.
    The itsy bitsy spider / retold by Iza Trapani.
        p.   cm.
    Summary: The itsy bitsy spider encounters a fan, a mouse, a cat,
and a rocking chair as she makes her way to the top of a tree to
spin her web.
    ISBN 1-879085-77-1
    [1. Spiders—Fiction.   2. Stories in rhyme.]   I. Title.
PZ8.3.T686It   1993
[E]—dc20   92-25150

The itsy bitsy spider
Climbed up the waterspout.

Down came the rain
And washed the spider out.

Out came the sun
And dried up all the rain,
And the itsy bitsy spider
Climbed up the spout again.

The itsy bitsy spider
Climbed up the kitchen wall.

Swoosh! went the fan
And made the spider fall.

Off went the fan.
No longer did it blow.
So the itsy bitsy spider
Back up the wall did go.

The itsy bitsy spider
Climbed up the yellow pail.

In came a mouse
And flicked her with his tail.

Down fell the spider.
The mouse ran out the door.
Then the itsy bitsy spider
Climbed up the pail once more.

The itsy bitsy spider
Climbed up the rocking chair.

Up jumped a cat
And knocked her in the air.

Down plopped the cat
And when he was asleep,
The itsy bitsy spider
Back up the chair did creep.

The itsy bitsy spider
Climbed up the maple tree.

She slipped on some dew
And landed next to me.

Out came the sun
And when the tree was dry,
The itsy bitsy spider
Gave it one more try.

The itsy bitsy spider
Climbed up without a stop.

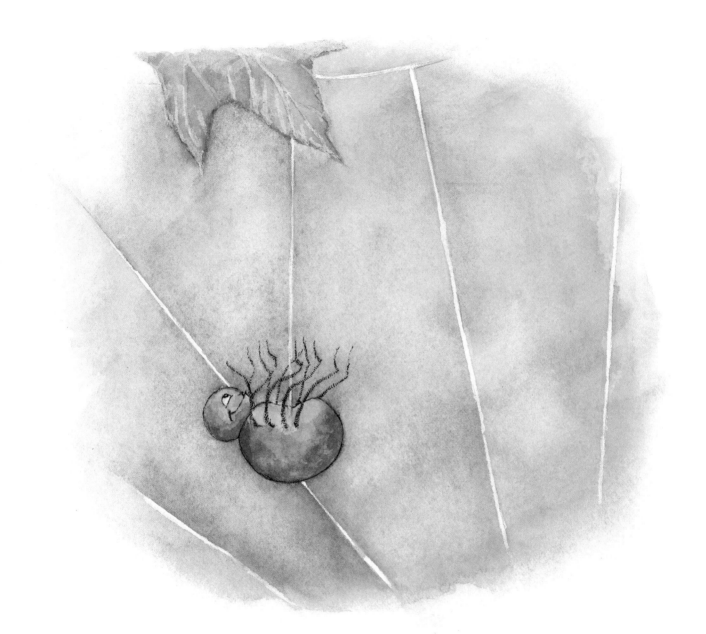

She spun a silky web
Right at the very top.

She wove and she spun
And when her web was done,

The itsy bitsy spider
Rested in the sun.

The it - sy bit - sy spi - der Climbed up the wa - ter - spout.

Down came the rain And washed the spi - der out.

Out came the sun And dried up all the rain, And the

it - sy bit - sy spi - der Climbed up the spout a - gain.

2. The itsy bitsy spider
   Climbed up the kitchen wall.
   Swoosh! went the fan
   And made the spider fall.
   Off went the fan.
   No longer did it blow.
   So the itsy bitsy spider
   Back up the wall did go.

3. The itsy bitsy spider
   Climbed up the yellow pail.
   In came a mouse
   And flicked her with his tail.
   Down fell the spider.
   The mouse ran out the door.
   Then the itsy bitsy spider
   Climbed up the pail once more.

4. The itsy bitsy spider
   Climbed up the rocking chair.
   Up jumped a cat
   And knocked her in the air.
   Down plopped the cat
   And when he was asleep,
   The itsy bitsy spider
   Back up the chair did creep.

5. The itsy bitsy spider
   Climbed up the maple tree.
   She slipped on some dew
   And landed next to me.
   Out came the sun
   And when the tree was dry,
   The itsy bitsy spider
   Gave it one more try.

6. The itsy bitsy spider
   Climbed up without a stop.
   She spun a silky web
   Right at the very top.
   She wove and she spun
   And when her web was done,
   The itsy bitsy spider
   Rested in the sun.